Happy [illegible]

Grandma Kitty

This book is dedicated to children and dogs everywhere who teach us to celebrate our lives through random acts of caring, kindness, and compassion.

Our lives gain a true sense of importance because of them.

Down, Bailey!

Thank You!

Brushes of the Heart

For other information, e-mail all inquiries to: info@riverrunbookstore.com

Published by Piscataqua Press
142 Fleet Street | Portsmouth, New Hampshire 03801 | USA

Printed in the United States of America

ISBN: 978-1-939739-38-4

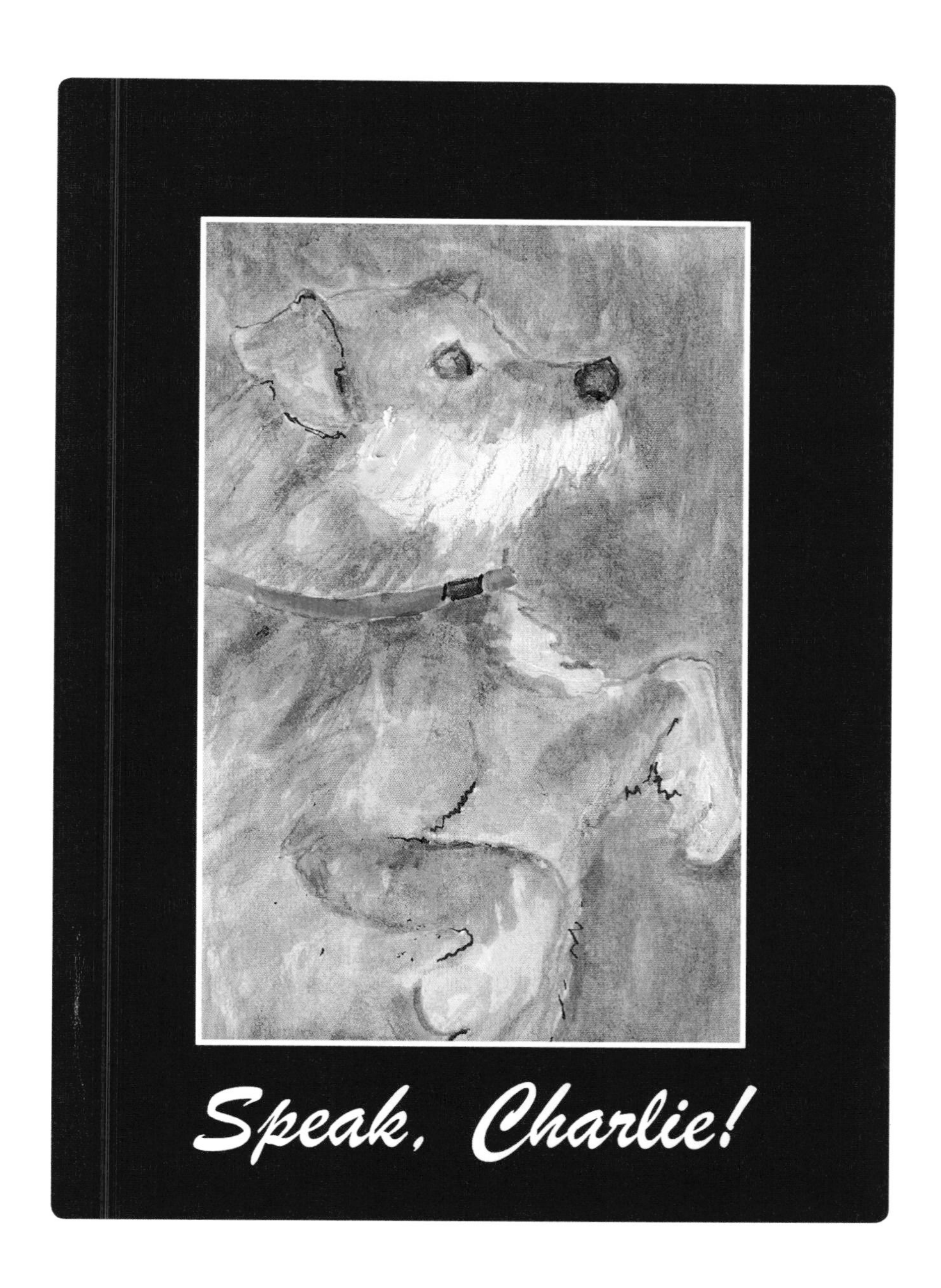
Speak, Charlie!

Brushes of the Heart

Story & Pictures by Ditty Mulry

The early morning air was filled with heat. Ditty closed her eyes and sat very still. In a bit of time an idea crept into her brain. That's it, she thought. "Mac, I'm going to roll this big white ball to you one more time and then we will go into the cabin to pack."

"Good," thought Mac as he plopped himself down into the green grass. "That white ball is so big and my legs are so little. I'm so exhausted!"

Inside the cabin, Ditty sat at her favorite desk to ponder what she should place in her suitcase. Paintbrushes, paint, paper, pencils, erasers. Endless thoughts raced through her head.

"Why Mac, you are all packed and waiting for Ditty. What a good doggie-boy. I see you've put on your red bossy breeches. I hope you packed your toothbrush."

Mac always drove the truck. Have you ever seen a doggie-boy drive a truck? Watch out, he might honk his horn at you!

The trip to the farm always took what seemed like forever, but Ditty never minded.

She spent her time gazing out the window at the ever-changing landscape. Billowing white clouds floated above on a backdrop of ultramarine blue sky. They reminded her of scoops of vanilla ice cream.

Distant mountains of lavenders and blues with unmown fields of golden grasses catching breaths of the warm summer wind. Ditty was lost in the sound of the silence.

"When will we be at the farm?" she heard Mac ask.

Ditty replied in a rest-filled voice: "Oh, from now till then."

The countryside was dotted with barns and silos waiting to be filled with hay. The sun was high in the sky and the cows were resting in the cool shade under some trees.

"Mac, there's the Battenkill," said Ditty as she watched the sun glisten on the water, making it sparkle as it flowed down the stream.

They reached the covered bridge and the boards rattled as the truck goes through.

"Oh Mac, we're here!" said Ditty in a voice filled with anticipation. "The barn door is open, so they're home."

The brightly colored zinnias along the stone wall nodded in a cheerful hello.

Mac parked the truck and they walked towards the house, passing the delphiniums dressed in shades of lavender and standing at a welcoming attention.

Ditty and Mac found Grandma seated in her garden enjoying the flowers. "Don't get up, Grandma" said Ditty as she raced to give her a hug.

Just then Grandpa came up from his vegetable garden carrying a basket of peas, Ditty's favorite! "Mac, there's Peter!"

Peter and Mac spent the days racing through the fields and meadows only stopping for a cool drink of water.

"Thank you, Mac, for getting Peter a drink. He sure is thirsty."

Each morning Ditty would go outside, set up her easel and begin to paint.

The farm was a very special place as it held memories dearto her heart.

On good days dinner was eaten outdoors on the picnic table. One evening Grandpa turned to Ditty and said "I think you and Mac should take a ride over to see Mr. Wilson." Ditty looked up from her plate and said, "Yes, Grandpa."

Peter and Mac have
finally decided to take
a rest in the hammock.

"Mac, don't squash Peter!"

The morning air was crisp and cool when Mac and Ditty climbed into the truck. "Mac, let's go down through Shushan. We haven't been that way for awhile."

Clunk-a-dee-clunk went the truck over the dirt road. The cows were out to pasture and Ditty caught a glimpse of Farmer Steele heading into his barn. A farmyard is always cluttered up with machinery and this and that thought Ditty. You can just tell farmers are busy from dawn to dusk, walking to and fro with their boots, tracking farmyard dirt and mud. Ditty loved busy people who lived their lives creating for others in a quiet and unassuming way. Grandma would say "going about their business."

Down through Shushan the truck went and headed towards Salem. Mac's voice was heard to say, "How much farther?" and Ditty replied, "Oh, from here to thereabouts."

Mac took a right turn at the stop light and headed down towards Blind Buck Hollow. Ditty was a good traveler because looking was one of her favorite things to do.

The landscape had changed from open fields to woods. Everything about the mornings' drive was perfect, mostly because Ditty was with her best friend, Mac.

"Mac, we're here," Ditty exclaimed, her voice filled with excitement. Mac took a left down Mr. Wilson's driveway as Ditty peered out the front window, taking everything in. Up ahead was Mr. Wilson, standing in his shed waving a big hello. Mac parked the truck, Ditty unlatched the door, hopped off the seat and ran to Mr. Wilson.

"Hi, Mr. Wilson. We're glad to see you."

"Hi, Ditty, I could hear the rattle of the truck, and Mac, you honked your horn," Mr. Wilson chuckled.

Ditty looked around to see two chickens and a duck, and next to Mr. Wilson was a small dog standing very still like a statue. "Oh, Mr. Wilson, what a cute dog. Do you have any more?"

"Yup, got one in the chicken coop."

Ditty and Mac followed Mr. Wilson where she spotted a furry matted ball with a wagging tail. Ditty opened the cage, reached in and gently took the doggie-girl into her arms and held her shaking body. "Oh my," said Ditty as she looked over and saw there was a horned owl in the adjoining cage.

Mr. Wilson looked down and said, "You can have her if you want." Ditty looked at Mr. Wilson and said, "Yes, Mr. Wilson," and hugged the doggie-girl.

Ditty looked down at her new little friend and gave her a gentle squeeze all the while wondering what to do. "I know," thought Ditty, "I'll bring her back to Grandma and Grandpa's and give her a bath." She shared her thoughts with Mr. Wilson, gave him a big hug and they said their good-byes.

Ditty

Mac drove the truck slowly, making sure not to hit too many bumps and divots. He didn't even honk his horn to signal good-bye to Mr. Wilson as he left his driveway.

On the way back to the farm, Ditty was very quiet and never looked up to see a horse in the field nodding to them in passing. Mac stopped in the middle of the dirt road to let a gaggle of geese stroll to the other side. He did not beep his horn. Good boy, Mac.

After what seemed like a very long truck ride the three friends arrived back at the farm.

Ditty filled a tub
with warm water
and proceeded to scrub
the doggie-girl clean. "Oh,
Peter, you brought a towel.
What a good boy. Are you napping?"

Ditty dried the doggie-girl with the towel. "Oh, my," said Ditty. "You look so very neat and smart. I think I'll call you Natty." And with that she gave Natty a big hug.

"Mac, thank you for giving Natty one of your doggie bones."

Our lives are like a work of art,
painted with brushes of the heart.

"Good night, Penny."

The End

Good fetch, Conor!

CPSIA information can be obtained
at www.ICGtesting.com
Printed in the USA
BVXC01n1612011014
368442BV00001B/1